Anonymous

Elias Warner Leavenworth

Anonymous

Elias Warner Leavenworth

ISBN/EAN: 9783744669559

Printed in Europe, USA, Canada, Australia, Japan

Cover: Foto ©Raphael Reischuk / pixelio.de

More available books at **www.hansebooks.com**

Elias Warner Leavenworth.

Born December Twenty, Eighteen Hundred and Three.

Died November Twenty-four, Eighteen Hundred and Eighty-seven.

MEMORIAL

DAY by day Death levels his unerring shaft and the victims fall about us so rapidly in these populous cities, that we become almost familiar with his visage, almost callous to his blows. And it is the ruling law of humanity that only here and there and at comparatively long intervals of time, one among the many is stricken down, whose loss is not only a private, but a public, calamity, whose place it is difficult, if not impossible, to fill, and whose life and character stand forth in the blazing light that falls upon us all in these modern days, with scarcely a visible flaw; a character so builded by himself and God's favor as to command the respect, the homage, and the admiration of his contemporaries. So the many must fall at the end of the race, with their worthy deeds, numerous though they be, known only to the limited circle wherein they were confined by the ordinary character of their natural endowments and the circumstances of birth and after-years; while the few, the very few, coming before the world blessed with God-given genius, talent, lofty purposes, perseverance, strength of will, and all the noble attributes which only can produce the perfect man, lay down their broken armor

5

on the conquered field of life, and not only their near and dear, but communities and their governing powers, the councils of the State and the nation, all feel a heavier burden, the loss of the guiding hand, the absence of the powerful yet benignant influence of the master-mind, and sorrow stretches abroad her somber wings.

To this latter class belonged, in a pre-eminent sense, he to whose memory the brief tribute of these pages is devoted—ELIAS WARNER LEAVENWORTH. His was a mind so generously endowed, his body so nobly constituted, his character so securely founded on the best and broadest principles of humanity and thereupon so moulded and builded by his own native powers and high purposes, that the whole structure, in the ripeness of years, was looked upon by all who knew him, with the highest respect and esteem.

The record of his long and busy life—a life filled to the fullest measure with private and public duties ably and successfully performed—can be easily written down; but it is a far more difficult task to so write of him that one may see and understand and appreciate his nobility of character, the gentle traits of his disposition, his broad unselfishness, the innate determination of his soul to so act toward his fellows, whether high or low, as to satisfy his own exacting conscience and entitle him to the proud name of a good man. These attributes of his inner self were best known, of course, only to those who enjoyed his confidence and companionship to an unusual degree, and can not be adequately described. But there is a cloud of witnesses, particularly in the city of his home, who in very many ways felt the beneficial influence of his wise counsel, his heartfelt sympathy in dark hours, the rich benison of his kindness, his benevolence, generosity, and unfailing goodness: these were the beautiful qualities

qualities that seemed to imbue his every act and shed radiance upon his daily life. To him the distinctions often recognized in humanity were meaningless, when his good offices were required. The step from the highest to the lowliest was insignificant to him, and among the multitudinous duties of his daily life none, however high and powerful, could so engross his time and thoughts, that others, however poor and humble, would not always find him with open ear for their needs and a hand ready for their aid. This broad human sympathy was a prominent trait in his character and extended into the dim by-ways of charity in a thousand deeds that are almost, if not entirely, unknown except to the recipients.

In close relationship with the characteristics mentioned, and springing from his recognition of the universal brotherhood of humanity, grew up his kindly tolerance of others; but this tolerance was never so broad as to cover the willful commission of a wrong of any kind. The soul of integrity himself, he could not and would not patiently tolerate the slightest departure from it in others. To him dishonesty of every description was crime, and crime of every degree he condemned to the uttermost. Between right and wrong he ever saw the great gulf; in his sight right was absolute right, and wrong was absolute wrong, and he felt that the dividing line between them was so clearly drawn that only the wilfully blind could fail to see it under all circumstances. His ideal of honor and justice between man and man was the highest, and earnest effort on the part of others to live up to such an ideal, whatever might be the results of such efforts, never failed to command his respect and aid. Governed as he was by a lofty creed of integrity, it is not a marvel that he was called by his fellow citizens to many high positions, while in the city where he lived, almost every public enterprise of any prominence and innumerable private trusts, were wholly or partially placed in his hands.

Mr. Leavenworth's collegiate education, supplemented by his natural tastes and liberal reading, gave him a decided love for, and appreciation of literary work of a high order. His critical judgment of such work was excellent, and outside of the busy paths of his daily business and public life he found time to exercise his mind and gratify his tastes in this regard in many ways. Education he believed to be the keystone of character and the only sure source of the highest achievements, and much of his time and means were devoted to its advancement. So with his love for the beautiful in nature and art—it was never chilled or suffered to lie dormant through the almost incessant and engrossing practical demands upon his time. Through his marvellous capacity and perfect method for accomplishing a vast amount of labor. which to many would have been appalling, he was enabled to fill out the æsthetic side of his life and gratify his artistic instincts. He possessed a comprehensive knowledge of botany and horticulture, and the adornment of his own home, especially its surrounding grounds ; his devotion to beautifying the lovely spot where his body was laid to rest : his untiring efforts to add to the attractiveness of the city where he lived, by the establishment of parks, planting of trees, and in various other ways, all testify to his love for the beautiful.

In the intimacies of love and friendship and in the bright circle of social and home life, Mr. Leavenworth found, undoubtedly, his happiest hours. His commanding presence. that any might envy, was accompanied by that habitual courtliness, modest grace and politeness that mark the refined and considerate gentleman, not of the "old school" alone, but of every school ; while his ready flow of intelligent conversation upon a broad range of subjects, his interest in the passing affairs of others, all contributed a charm to his personality that made him most welcome in every social assemblage and drew across his own threshold the steps of innumerable friends and acquaintances, as well as many who were high in the councils of the country.

By the side of his own hearthstone Mr. Leavenworth's daily life was the beautiful example of devotion, unselfishness, patience, and thoughtful care that would be expected from such a character and that never fail to constitute the ideal home. No detail of domestic duty was too insignificant to command his attention if it was desired, and over and through all shone the pure sunlight of an unfailing love.

In Mr. Leavenworth's nature was a strong religious element, and thereupon was grounded a faith that remained unshaken by any of the transitions and plausible theories of skepticism that have disturbed the otherwise calm sea of christianity in recent times. For the greater share of his life he was an active officer and member of the church he loved and helped to rear ; and, moreover, it was his belief that a man's daily deeds should reflect his religion and constitute a part of it, and while he shrank from all ostentatious display of convictions and observances that he held sacred, he was yet continually sustained by the unfaltering faith that enabled him to serenely meet all of life's struggles, and carried him down to the shores of the dark river in tranquility and peace.

> " Why weep ye thus for him who, having run
>   The bound of man's appointed years, at last,
> Life's blessings all enjoyed, life's labours done,
>   Serenely to his final rest has passed :
> While the soft memory of his virtues yet
> Lingers, like twilight hues, when the bright sun has set."

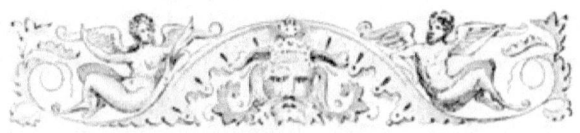

ELIAS WARNER LEAVENWORTH was born in Canaan, Columbia county, New York, on the 20th day of December, 1803. His ancestry is traced back to Thomas Leavenworth, of England, who emigrated to America a little before 1670. In the fifth generation from Thomas was born David Leavenworth, who was the father of Elias Warner. David was born in what is now Watertown, Conn., September 12, 1769, and was married to Lucinda Mather, at Torringford, Conn., January 16, 1794. He was a physician in early life and, after two years of practice, settled in New Canaan. Three years later, his large practice having injured his health, he secured the appointment of State printer and went to Albany and formed the firm of Leavenworth and Whiting, booksellers and stationers. In 1803 a change in political affairs deprived him of the State printing and he returned to New Canaan, whence he removed, in 1806, to Great Barrington, Mass., and engaged in mercantile business with his youngest brother, Isaac. The remainder of his life until his death, on the 25th of May, 1831, was passed in Great Barrington. In the family genealogy* it is recorded that "he was a man of high personal character, an active and consistent member of

---

*Published by the subject of this sketch in 1873.

the Congregational church, of unquestioned integrity, great firmness of purpose, and strong, active, and vigorous powers of mind. He was energetic and public spirited, and took a prominent part in every enterprise for the improvement of the town. He was repeatedly a member of the Legislature, in the high political time of 1812-13, and for many years before his death was Moderator of the town. On the 18th of June, 1819, he was appointed one of the Justices of the Peace within and for the county of Berkshire for seven years from that date, 'if he should so long behave himself well in said office.' His life was one of great activity and usefulness and he died in the full enjoyment of the love and respect of his neighbors and fellow-citizens, and with perfect trust in the mercy of his Savior."

The early life of Elias Warner Leavenworth, until he was sixteen years of age, was passed, as he wrote, "among the beautiful hills and valleys of Berkshire." During the year 1819 he attended the academy at Hudson, N. Y., a reputable institution then under the care of Rev. Mr. Parker, (whose son subsequently became Judge Amasa J. Parker,) and in the fall of 1820 he entered Williams College as a sophomore. At that time he was prepared to enter Yale as a freshman and had intended to do so, but was persuaded to give one year to Williams, which was then passing through a critical period of her history. In the fall of 1821 he entered Yale as a sophomore, graduated with honor in 1824, and took his second degree in 1827. Thus was fulfilled his early determination to secure a thorough education, which he always held to be the most valuable acquisition for a young man *

---

* At a late year in his life Mr. Leavenworth wrote as follows: "A thorough education is an almost indispensable requisite to any valuable success in life, and to the accomplishment of any great good. It is an investment which its possessor can never lose. It is an unfailing source of pride and perennial enjoyment, the foundation for extended usefulness, the means through which an honorable support may be secured, and which brings out into the fullest development all the latent powers and energies of the man."

11

Having decided to adopt the legal profession, Mr. Leavenworth began its study on his twenty-first birth-day, December 20, 1824, in the office of the late William Cullen Bryant, who was then practicing in Great Barrington, and on the 16th day of May, 1825, he entered the law school at Litchfield, Conn., then under direction of the Hon. James Gould. He remained there until January, 1827, when he was admitted to practice in all the courts of Connecticut. Too close application to study had at this time affected Mr. Leavenworth's eyes, and he passed the spring, summer, and autumn of that year in the office of Increase Sumner, giving little attention to his profession.

In the summer of the same year (1827) the late Hon. Joshua A. Spencer, then of Utica, visited Mr. Leavenworth's father, in Great Barrington, and under his advice Mr. Leavenworth determined to settle in Syracuse. Accordingly, on the 12th day of November, 1827, he started for his new home. Means of travel were not then what they now are, and it was only by exercising diligence that he reached Syracuse a week later. He entered the struggling village on a canal boat and found a hamlet of a few buildings only, and giving very little promise of its subsequent greatness.

On reaching Syracuse Mr. Leavenworth began study and practice with Alfred Northram, which continued until February, 1829, when the late B. Davis Noxon removed to Syracuse in consequence of the removal of the courts from Onondaga Hill. A partnership was formed between him and Mr. Leavenworth, and the latter was associated with some member of the Noxon family until the year 1850. The successive firm names of which Mr. Leavenworth was a member were : Noxon & Leavenworth, Noxons, Leavenworth & Comstock (formed by the addition of Geo. F. Comstock and Geo. W. Noxon); then Noxon, Leavenworth

12

& Comstock (George Noxon having died, his father having retired, and James Noxon coming into the firm); and, lastly, of Noxon & Leavenworth again.

Mr. Leavenworth's legal career was eminently successful and extended down to the year 1850. It was marked by industry of the most persevering character, while his power of impressing courts and juries with his views of important cases, a power that was continually strengthened with passing years, gave him early prominence in the bar. Had he been physically able and inclined to follow the profession, it is quite safe to assume that he would eventually have occupied a place among the foremost legal minds of the time. But the state of his health in the year 1850 rendered it imperative that he should abandon practice. In addition to his work in court, he labored arduously during the great political campaign of 1840, speaking almost daily to large audiences, which brought on an attack of bronchitis which, at the time of his retirement, had rendered his condition somewhat critical ; and although then in the enjoyment of, perhaps, a larger and more lucrative business in the courts of central New York than any other attorney, he was forced to abandon it. It had been his uniform practice to remain in his office until eleven o'clock at night and he had taxed his energies to the utmost ; but rest and care during the succeeding two or three years fully restored his health and strength.

Mr. Leavenworth's twenty years residence in Syracuse had already firmly established him in a foremost position in the confidence and esteem of the community, and had long before been the recipient of the first of that long series of public trusts and offices which he was destined to fill. As early as January, 1832, he was appointed a Lieutenant of Artillery in the 147th regiment of infantry, and later in the same year was commissioned Cap-

13

tain of Artillery in the same regiment. In 1834 he was appointed Lieutenant-Colonel of the 29th regiment of artillery, and in the following year was promoted to Colonel of the same regiment. This rapid series of promotions was still farther advanced in the year 1836, when he was appointed Brigadier-General of the 7th brigade of artillery (thus acquiring the military title by which he was almost universally known), which high military honor he enjoyed until the year 1841, when he voluntarily resigned the office. In a military capacity the same qualifications that gave him success in other fields, combined with a lofty and dignified bearing and the genius to command, made him a model and popular officer whose value was appreciated by the community and the State.

In the fall of the year 1835, General Leavenworth was nominated by the Whig county convention as one of the four members of Assembly from Onondaga ; but, as he has naively recorded, "the county was hopelessly Democratic, or he would not have consented to be a candidate." In 1837 he was appointed a Trustee of the village of Syracuse, and in 1838 was elected President of the village, which office he held until the spring of 1841.

General Leavenworth had by this time cultivated a rugged faith in the future of his adopted home, and shown an interest in everything that promised to advance its welfare, which inspired his fellow citizens with the belief that they could find no fitter person to head its government. While he was President of the village, from 1838 to 1841, the Board of Trustees opened and extended many of the streets which are now among the most prominent in the city. Of these were Warren street, opened from Jefferson south to Salina street, a substantial bridge being built across the Yellow Brook at the point where Warren street

14

is intersected by Madison. During the year 1838 the Syracuse and Utica railroad company applied for the privilege of locating their depot on Washington street, between Salina and Warren streets, to cover a width of forty-nine feet. The Board declined to grant the request, although favorable to it; but a public meeting was called for the action of the citizens, to be held at the Syracuse House, on the 26th of December, 1838. On the evening, General Leavenworth drew up the resolution, which was adopted by the meeting, giving to the city what is now Vanderbilt Square, the rows of trees which still line each side of the railroad from Beech street to the heart of the city, and the first public sewer that reached the Yellow Brook. It compelled the railroad company to buy twenty-six feet off from the north end of the block south of the depot, and four feet off from the north end.

Previous to 1839 the Geneva turnpike ran diagonally from northeast to southwest through the grounds now constituting Fayette Park. General Leavenworth, while President of the village, drew up and succeeded in obtaining the passage of a bill discontinuing the road at that point and thus securing the beautiful park which is now the especial pride of that portion of the city.

These were the beginnings of that long series of public acts performed by General Leavenworth, which contributed so much toward making Syracuse what it is to-day. His watchful, observant eye seldom overlooked a needed improvement of any description, and there was none more ready than he to devote valuable time and money to any object that promised to benefit or beautify the city.

In 1839 General Leavenworth was elected Supervisor of the old town of Salina, then the largest town in the State and embracing the four incorporated villages of Syracuse, Salina, Liverpool and Geddes. He was re-elected to that office in 1840. In 1846 and 1847 he was again chosen President of the village. During this term the Board, at his suggestion, took possession of the two pieces of ground, then unoccupied, now known as Warren and Ashland parks, fenced them in and set trees about them.

In the year 1849 General Leavenworth served his first term as Mayor of the young city of Syracuse, and in this office he exercised the same wise foresight he had already exhibited for the improvement of the growing place. The tract of land of which Armory park is now the center, was laid out under his direction on what was then State lands. A map of the tract was made, which he took before the Land Commission at Albany, whom he influenced to consent to a sale of the tract, upon certain conditions favorable to the city, thus securing another park.

In the fall of 1849 General Leavenworth was elected to the Legislature to represent the city district. He was there made chairman of the committee on the manufacture of salt and a member of the committee on railroads. The members of the Legislature were at that time bitterly prejudiced against Onondaga salt, chiefly through ignorance of its merits, and disposed to remove the tolls from foreign salt when transported over the canals. General Leavenworth threw the weight of his influence and his most earnest efforts into the discussion of the subject and finally had the satisfaction of seeing every vestige of prejudice removed and the tolls allowed to remain. He drew a bill, (laws 1850, chap. 374, p. 794,) on the subject which was passed by the Legislature.

The general railroad law of the State was reported from the committee of which he was a member, but was violently opposed by several of the ablest members of the Legislature. The chief support of this bill devolved upon General Leavenworth, he being the only ready debater on the committee. The bill was most ably discussed, the Committee of the Whole holding nine separate sittings upon it ; but in spite of the able and active opposition it received, its friends had the satisfaction of seeing it passed. General Leavenworth's influence also carried through the Legislature the bill for the improvement of Seneca river (chap. 153, laws 1850,) against two elaborate speeches by the late Gov. Raymond, then the ablest speaker in the House. For his work in favor of this bill General Leavenworth received the warmest congratulations of his colleagues and constituents. These were measures of great importance to the State at large and form a conspicuous portion of the legislative labor accomplished by General Leavenworth, the effects of which are still felt.

It was during this term in the Legislature, also, that General Leavenworth was called upon by a delegation of gentlemen from the village of Newburg, to lend his powerful aid in favor of the bill for the preservation of Washington's Headquarters, it having failed in the hands of the original Select Committee. He moved the reference of the bill, which was still in existence, to a new committee late in the session, the resolution was adopted, and a committee of his own selection appointed. The bill was then remodeled and objectionable parts stricken out, when General Leavenworth, as chairman of the committee, reported it and it passed without difficulty. This action preserves for all posterity one of the most interesting historical landmarks in the country.

The celebrated "Mason Will Case" was also before the House in that year. This long-contested case had passed through the courts, which had sustained the will, the affirmation of the Supreme Court judgment being effected in the Court of Appeals by a tie vote. The bill appeared to be an innocent one and on its face merely provided that the Court of Appeals should grant a rehearing on all judgments by affirmance by a tie vote between two certain dates. Upon examination, however, it appeared that there was but one such case between the dates mentioned and that was the Mason Will Case. It was, therefore, a law by which a rehearing was to be granted by the Legislature in a case finally decided by the Court of Appeals. We quote from General Leavenworth's record of the subsequent action on this bill as follows: "It had passed the House without any notice or any question being raised and the Governor had sent down his veto. I had been urgently requested on both sides to take part on the veto, and declined. But, to my utter astonishment, when the question came before the house the veto had a *very* feeble support and many of the best men and even the best lawyers in the House attacked it. I sat quietly in my seat as long as it was possible. But the bill seemed to me such an outrage, such an usurpation of the province of the Court, that I could not remain silent. I entered into the debate with all the zeal of my nature and all the powers I could exert, and made speech after speech. A large audience listened to the argument. After a long and highly exciting debate the friends of the bill failed to over-ride the veto by only a single vote."

Those who knew General Leavenworth's nature, his hatred of wrong and imposition, and his manner of encountering them, will readily bring to mind his probable appearance and action on that occasion. It was possible for him, when required, to overwhelm his antagonists with invective as well as logic, and to brush them away by the mere force of his personality, and it may be imagined that he did so in this instance.

There existed for many years a firm friendship between General Leavenworth and Thurlow Weed, the eminent politician, a friendship that was enhanced by the latter's earlier relations with Judge Joshua Forman, (Mrs. Leavenworth's father,) in whose family Mr. Weed resided for some time when a boy. On several occasions Mr. Weed used his great political influence in General Leavenworth's interest, and after Gov. Fish had, in 1850, offered the General the vacancy in the office of State Comptroller (occasioned by the resignation of Washington Hunt) which offer General Leavenworth could not accept on account of his still being a Member of the Legislature, he was tendered through Mr. Weed the nomination for either Attorney-General or Judge of the Court of Appeals. This flattering offer he declined, owing to his firm determination to not again connect himself in any way with the legal profession.

At the time this offer was made, General Leavenworth was brought forward by his immediate friends, as candidate for the office of Secretary of State. This action was independent of the ruling political powers at Albany and of Mr. Weed's potent agency, yet he lacked only six or eight votes of securing the nomination.

In the fall of 1853 General Leavenworth was nominated for Secretary of State, almost without opposition and probably at Mr. Weed's suggestion. During his term in this high office he exercised his habitual industry and his efforts were, as usual productive of a vast amount of good. For example, he and Gen. James M. Cook were appointed a Building Committee by the Commissioners of the Land Office, to take down the old State Hall in Albany, and erect the building known as the State Agricultural Rooms and Cabinet of Natural History. They were also the Building Committee for the extension of the Capitol and the extensive refitting and refurnishing of the Assembly chamber.

During the year 1855, with aid of Franklin B. Hough, then chief clerk of the Census Department of the State, General Leavenworth superintended the taking of the census, personally appointing about two thousand marshals, drawing up the blank forms, superintending the printing and its distribution to every part of the State, and giving the needed explanations and instructions to the marshals through the medium of from one hundred and fifty to two hundred letters daily for several weeks—a most arduous task, but performed with the accuracy and efficiency that characterized his every public act.

During the period just referred to, General Leavenworth accomplished a service which conferred great benefit upon the citizens of Syracuse, which he modestly described as follows : "The State, in 1854, owned that part of the city of Syracuse lying west of Plum street, north of the Erie canal, east of Van Rensselaer street and south of the salt water reservoir, and a portion of Onondaga creek. These lands were then used for the manufacture of solar salt. The removal of the coarse salt works having been ordered by the Commissioners of the Land Office from those portions of this tract lying on the east side of West Genesee street, 16 rods in depth, the Commissioners, at my suggestion and solicitation, resolved to survey out and map the whole tract and appointed me to supervise and direct in regard to it. This was done under and by virtue of chapter 391 of the laws of 1864, p. 986. I caused it to be laid out substantially as it now appears on the maps, straightening West Genesee street, laying out the lots on each side 100 feet front and sixteen rods deep, making the second class streets 80 feet wide, instead of 66, as they are in other parts of the city : laying out a park near the center of the tract just as large as the Commissioners would sanction, surrounded by ample lots and with a broad avenue 120 feet wide leading from this park to the vacant and State lands near the pump house. When the map of the tract was sanctioned by the Commissioners and laid before the Common Council of the city, they did me the honor to give my name to both the park and the avenue."

Whatever public duties were pressed upon his attention (and they were, for many years, too numerous to recount here) and whatever the tax upon his time and his energies, it will thus be seen that General Leavenworth never neglected or overlooked an opportunity to serve the city of his home. It appeared to be constantly in his thoughts and we can think of him in this regard only as continually watchful and observant, not only that he might be ever ready to do what it was generally acknowledged should be done, but to discover opportunities for improvements which had been entirely overlooked by others.

Another important service to the State (perhaps the most important single public act of his life as far as the State of New York is concerned) was also performed in 1854 and resulted in the final completion, through the labors of Prof. James Hall, of his great work on our Natural History. When General Leavenworth entered upon the duties of his office on the first of January of that year the Natural History had been carried as far as the second volume of the Paleontology and there it had been decided to leave it, after an expenditure of about $600,000. The folly of such a course and its great injustice to Professor Hall, deeply impressed General Leavenworth and he determined the great work should be finished. He accordingly conferred with the Hon. Samuel Blatchford, of New York, then Chairman of the Committee of Ways and Means, in the House, and with the Hon. Henry Raymond, then Lieutenant-Governor, who entered into his views relative to the work and promised their aid. Owing to the large amount of money already expended on the work and the lack of popular appreciation of the scientific value of the Paleontology, the subject was an unpopular one in the Legislature. With his accustomed foresight, General Leavenworth saw that it would not answer to trust to a separate bill, and although money was not immediately needed for the work he turned to the appropriation bill as the surest avenue to success. A section was therefore inserted in the bill, "appropriating $5,000 for the payment of any expenses growing out of the Natural History of the State, to be applied only on the certificate of the Secretary of State and the Secretary of the Board of Regents, who are hereby authorized and directed to take charge of all the matters appertaining to the compilation and *completion* of such Natural History, with power to make such contracts, limiting the number of volumes, and fixing the compensation, and otherwise as they may think proper." It will be seen that under the skillful wording of this act the most sweeping powers were conferred, and in such a way that the opponents of the Natural History saw nothing in it to alarm them. The provision was passed without opposition. Knowing the large interests involved and the subject embracing so much of a technical character, General Leavenworth (upon whom almost the entire responsibility of the arrangements fell) invited Prof. Agassiz, Messrs. Gould, Dana and Dr. Dewey to meet him at Albany for a conference, an invitation which they readily accepted. There and in General Leavenworth's active brain at a subsequent time was completed every detail of the arrangements and plans, which need not be entered into here, for the completion by Prof. Hall of the great work which bears his name.

By virtue of his office as Secretary of State, General Leavenworth was *ex-officio* visitor to the charitable institutions of the

State. As he, in this relation, at once made himself more familiar than he had before been with the condition of these institutions, he saw the urgent need of some superior investigating and supervising power which would of necessity visit and inspect them annually, investigate the details of their management, the expenditure of the appropriations made for them, and other kindred matters, and report to the Legislature. For supplying this need, General Leavenworth drew a bill, which was introduced in the Senate on the 31st of January, 1855, entitled, " An Act entitled an act in relation to charitable institutions supported or assisted by the State, and to City and County Poor Houses, and to create a Board of Visitors for the same." The bill was favorably reported and sent to the Committee of the Whole, but was not disposed of in that year, except by a resolution that the president of the Senate should appoint a committee of three to examine into the affairs of all such institutions, obtain full information, etc. In the Legislature of 1867 the subject was again agitated and the Hon. Charles S. Hoyt, then Chairman of the Committee on Charitable Institutions, applied to General Leavenworth for a copy of his original bill. With his customary methodical care he had preserved it and it was sent as requested ; it became almost literally the law as it passed the Legislature of that year.

It is a pleasure to record any of the public acts of General Leavenworth, and especially those wherein he was able to exhibit his loyalty and devotion to the city of his home. One of these opportunities was offered him in the matter of the location of the New York State Asylum for Idiots. In the year 1855 the trustees of the asylum purchased five acres of land on the Troy road near Albany, as a site for the institution. This site was so undesirable that the Senator from Albany caused a provision to

23

be inserted in the appropriation bill, authorizing the trustees to sell or exchange the land. A committee was appointed under this provision, consisting of General Leavenworth and two others, to examine the vicinity of Albany for a more desirable site and report. It was reported that no better site could be found in that vicinity. General Leavenworth submitted, with the report, a long and elaborate argument against any site near Albany and accompanied it by an offer signed by about twenty citizens of Syracuse to give without charge any ten acres of ground near that city, or pay the trustees $7,500 in cash, provided the institution was located at Syracuse. This action on the part of the twenty citizens, as may have been supposed, was brought about solely by General Leavenworth, who had before invited them to meet him at his office, where the matter was arranged. The offer led to a very animated discussion in the Legislature. The removal was favored by Gov. Seymour and also by Hon. John C. Spencer, president of the board of trustees, who, with General Leavenworth, were made the Committee to superintend the erection of the new buildings. The removal was voted for by almost every member of the House.

We have before briefly referred to General Leavenworth's cultivated literary tastes and the high character of his purely intellectual attainments. Throughout his life, although it seems to have been filled with a continued succession of public and private trusts requiring arduous labor and a large portion of his time, he still found many hours which he devoted to a further cultivation of his intellectual faculties, to extensive reading and the studious ways of the scholar. His high intellectual rank was not unknown far beyond the circle of his general acquaintance. This is clearly indicated by his election on the 4th of January, 1855, as a Corresponding Member of the American Historical and Geographical Society of the city of New York, and his reception the same year of a similar honor by the New England Historical and Genealogical Society of Boston; also by his subsequent appointment as one of the Regents of the University of the State of New York, and his selection in 1864 to preside at the meeting of the Alumni of Yale College. At its Commencement in 1871, Hamilton College conferred upon him the honorary degree of Doctor of Laws. These honors were, perhaps, as keenly appreciated by him as any ever conferred upon him.

It will not be out of place here to mention the fact that General Leavenworth's researches in Genealogy had begun prior to the date under consideration, especially in that of his own name in this country. His labor in this direction continued with little interruption down to 1873, and involved the most extensive line of correspondence, reading and compilation ever given, perhaps, to the genealogy of any family. In 1873 he published the results of his long and patient research in a volume of nearly four hundred pages.

Returning to his public life in the order of its years, General Leavenworth was again elected to the Legislature in 1856. The position he then held in that body is shown by his appointment as Chairman of the Committee on Canals, as a member of the Committee on Banks, and particularly as Chairman of the Select Committee of one from each judicial district, on the equalization of the State tax. It is noteworthy that, in a large majority of the many occasions where he served on committees, he was given the chairmanship; though a fact of minor importance, it shows his natural capacity and fitness to lead, and that he was regarded by his fellows as one whose general competency and integrity deserved their highest recognition. This equalization committee was appointed on the 27th of January, and on the 31st of the same month General Leavenworth reported a bill, which he had himself drawn in the meantime, providing for the appointment of a Board of three State Assessors to equalize the tax. So important was this measure considered that it was discussed four successive days in Committee of the Whole, where it was violently opposed by representatives of the counties that would be most affected by its provisions; but it was sustained by a decisive majority, and on the 3d of April (as Chairman of a Committee to report important bills which should have preference and receive action before final adjournment) General Leavenworth reported that bill and the report was agreed to. At this time his health had become impaired by excessive labor and he was compelled to absent himself from his seat for several days, owing to which the bill was not then acted upon; but two years later it was again introduced and passed. It has ever since then been of immense benefit to the State. (Laws of 1859, chap. 312, p. 702, etc.)

During this session General Leavenworth also drew and introduced bills providing for investigation into the origin of fires in certain cases; to remove an evil from which country banks were suffering; several local bills pertaining to matters in Syracuse, but not of paramount importance, and a large number of others in the general course of legislation, relating to the canals, banks and other subjects. Such records of legislative labor performed by one man are almost unparalleled, and with the diverse tasks of many other public and private interests, it is not a wonder that his health suffered at times.

In the winter of 1858, Gov. John A. King sent General Leavenworth's name to the Senate for the office of Auditor of the State, but the then existing combination between the Democracy and the so-called Know-Nothings comprised a majority of the members, and the nomination was laid over until the succeeding

4th of July, when the Senate would not be in session. When Governor Morgan came into office in the following January, General Leavenworth withdrew in favor of Hon. Nathaniel S. Benton.

Referring again to General Leavenworth's public life in the city of Syracuse we must return to the year 1852, at which time the citizens were holding meetings and actively discussing the establishment of a rural cemetery; but no suitable grounds could then be decided upon and the undertaking languished until 1857, chiefly because there had no one volunteered to place himself at the head of the movement. In 1857 other meetings were held in relation to the matter, but in consequence of the financial trouble of that period, all efforts were again abandoned. In 1858 General Leavenworth and Hamilton White, having decided for themselves that a part of the present grounds was the most suitable to be obtained for a cemetery, they opened negotiations with the owner of twenty acres in the front and seventy-five acres in the rear part of the original purchase. The Syracuse and Jamesville plank road ran through this tract, and extended negotiations with the directors became necessary, and also with the Commissioners of Highways of the town and with David S. Colvin for land for a new route for the road. At the end of a year, and after many annoyances and the expenditure of much time and labor, the preliminaries were all settled and the terms agreed upon. It remained now to raise about $25,000 to fully accomplish the first part of the undertaking. In this task the aid of A. C. Powell was contributed and the necessary fund was soon raised and on the 15th of August the Association of Oakwood was organized and trustees elected. The next day the trustees chose General Leavenworth as president, A. C. Powell vice-president, Hamilton White, treasurer and Allen Munro,

27

secretary. The office of president was held by General Leavenworth as long as he lived and no one at all conversant with the facts will need to be told of his untiring devotion, his watchful care and oversight of every detail, and his faithful labor that beautiful Oakwood might be what it now is, one of the loveliest of all the lovely resting-places for the dead in the country. General Leavenworth loved its every pathway, mound and spreading tree as he did the shrubs and flowers of his own home-grounds and if he had never done a beneficent act other than the part he took in the establishment of this cemetery, the citizens of Syracuse would still be very deeply indebted to him.

In the spring of 1859 General Leavenworth was again elected Mayor of Syracuse. It was in this year that he induced the Common Council to order the sale of all that part of Rose Hill Cemetery upon which there had been no burials, being about ten acres. This tract was laid out under his direction, excepting a portion at the intersection of three streets, which was reserved and is now known as Highland Park—another of those playgrounds of the poor as well as of the rich, for which the dwellers in Syracuse are indebted to his foresight and cultivated taste. This was the fifth park in Syracuse which was secured directly through his efforts, none of which, it may be reasonably supposed, would have been otherwise provided; and ten years later he was instrumental in adding still another to the number by influencing the owners of the Prospect Hill tract, who had already filed their map, to so change it as to leave out to public use the Square that now beautifies that locality. If a man with such broad views can properly be said to have had a hobby, it was the universal need and the wisdom of establishing parks at every available spot in a city; and intimately associated with his views on this subject were his love for broad streets and his enthusiasm in setting out trees and inducing others to follow his example : and he insisted upon setting none but elm trees. They are more beautiful, longer-lived, cleaner, and more desirable every way than any other variety, and it was one of his most absorbing desires that every added street should be broad and lined with the beautiful elms. It would be interesting to know how many his own hands planted or helped to plant in the streets he loved so well.

In the fall of 1859, General Leavenworth was again nominated for the high office of Secretary of State ; but for reasons wholly political he was destined to defeat. The same combination before alluded to, in opposition to the Republicans, was successful, although he lacked less than 1,500 votes of election, in a poll of about 600,000.

In the winter of 1860, General Leavenworth was appointed by the Legislature, one of the Board of Quarantine Commissioners, and upon the organization of the Board was chosen its President. Most of the following summer he passed on Staten Island in the discharge of the duties of that office. In the summer of the same year he was chosen President of the Republican State Convention, then soon to assemble in Chicago. This high honor was accredited by him, in a large measure, to the intimate and friendly relations which had long existed between himself and William H. Seward.

On the 5th of February, 1861, General Leavenworth was chosen by the Legislature in joint ballot, one of the Regents of the University, an office to which he gave his most earnest efforts and with a degree of success that will be fully appreciated by reading the tributes of his colleagues upon the announcement of his death, which will be found on another of these pages. He occupied this station with distinguished honor until his death.

In March, 1861, General Leavenworth was nominated by the President of the United States, and confirmed by the Senate, as the Commissioner on the part of the United States, under the convention with New Granada, in which capacity he served until the commission expired in 1862. This appointment was one calling for diplomatic skill of a high order, as well as far-seeing financial judgment and sagacity. To the commission was referred all claims of American citizens and corporations from the foundation of the government of New Granada down to the time of the treaty, involving many millions of dollars.

In January, 1862, General Leavenworth was elected President of the Syracuse Savings Bank. He may be said to have been the founder of the savings bank business of Syracuse, as he assuredly was its most active promoter during the remainder of his life. Into the methods of management of that very successful financial institution he introduced the most perfect system and over its every investment he exercised a watchful care that soon gave it the confidence of the community and its business rapidly increased. At the time of his resignation, in 1883, the deposits of this bank had reached more than $2,000,000. Its magnificent building was erected during General Leavenworth's administration and is an object of just pride to all.

In the spring of 1865, General Leavenworth was made the President of the Board of Commissioners appointed by the Governor to locate the State Asylum for the Blind, which resulted in fixing on Batavia as the most eligible and desirable location for that beneficent institution. In the fall of the same year he was appointed by the Governor, a trustee of the State Asylum for Idiots, in the place of Hamilton White, deceased, and in January, 1866, was reappointed, with the concurrence of the Senate; this office he held until 1885.

In the summer of 1867, General Leavenworth was elected one of the trustees of Hamilton College, but was reluctantly compelled to decline the honor, as his office of Regent rendered him ineligible. In the same year he was also appointed by the Legislature a member of the Board of Commissioners, consisting of the Adjutant-General and the Inspector-General of the State, with himself, for the further improvement of the State Armory in Syracuse.

In May, 1868, General Leavenworth was appointed by the Legislature a member of a Board of Commissioners, of which he was chosen President, to establish a system of sewerage for the city of Syracuse. This Board was engaged two years in perfecting the system and all their maps, plans, etc., were filed in the city and county clerk's offices on the 7th of May, 1870. For the completion of the system at that time the city is directly indebted to General Leavenworth. He had seen and fully appreciated the necessity for the improvement, had often urged its importance, and finally drew up a bill, procured the calling of a public meeting and there submitted the bill, which was unanimously approved and finally became the law.

In the same year (1868) the Syracuse Home Association, an organization dating back to 1852, at which time General Leavenworth, Hamilton White and Thomas B. Fitch had raised by subscription between $12,000 and $15,000 as a partial endowment for the institution, sold their old home on East Fayette street. Moses D. Burnet had generously offered the Home a new site on the corner of Hawley and Townsend streets, on condition that the Board of Counselors should raise $25,000 for the construction of a new building. With his accustomed energy in all good works, General Leavenworth, in connection with Mr. Fitch, spent much of their time during several weeks and succeeded in

31

raising more than the required sum. This, with various sums raised by others, supplied a fund of more than $32,000. General Leavenworth was, of course, on the Building Committee of the new structure and was largely instrumental in giving to the city the attractive, commodious and vastly useful institution known as the " Old Ladies' Home."

On the 22d of November, 1872, General Leavenworth was honored with the appointment by the Governor of the State and the Senate as one of the thirty-two Commissioners (four from each Judicial District,) selected to amend the State Constitution. His colleagues in the Fifth District were Hon. Daniel Pratt, Hon. Francis Kernan and Hon. Ralph McIntosh. The commission met at Albany on December 4, 1872, and adjourned March 15, 1873, during which period the numerous important amendments to the constitution with which the public were made familiar at the time, were formulated and eventually became and now are a part of the foundation of the State government. Two of the more important amendments were introduced by General Leavenworth and he was chiefly responsible for them. One of them, the 14th section of the 7th article, applies to the statute of limitations to all claims against the State. The other is contained in the 10th and 11th sections of the 8th article and forbids the giving or loaning of the credit or money of the State, or of any city, town, or village, in a variety of cases specified. He was also prominently active in the preparation of other sections, notably that relating to savings banks and that limiting the powers of the Legislature in certain cases. Though his health was at that time delicate, he was more regular in attendance at the sessions of the Commission than almost any other member.

The numerous political honors which had been bestowed upon General Leavenworth culminated in the fall of 1874, when he received the nomination for Representative in Congress in the Twenty-fifth District. His majority in the ensuing election was most flattering to himself and his friends. Although now past the allotted term of man's life, when the intellectual and bodily powers of most men are seriously waning or beyond the capacity for useful work, General Leavenworth's Congressional career was of such a prominent and active character as to call for the highest commendation from his constituents. It was said of him by a prominent Republican journal near the close of his term that, "it is gratifying to know that General Leavenworth has taken a high position at Washington, that he is considered one of the most industrious and useful members of the House, and that no man in his first term could have a more honorable standing than that which he occupies. He has made a most excellent impression by his speeches in that body. Besides several briefer efforts he has spoken at length upon two subjects of general interest, viz., the Hawaiian Treaty and the Geneva Awards, both speeches being among the best delivered upon those subjects." At a later date, (the 25th of January, 1877,) near the close of his term, General Leavenworth made another lengthy and able speech, upon the counting of the Electoral Votes, a power which it was sought by his opponents to transfer from Congress to the Vice-president of the United States, a change that General Leavenworth and many other able men viewed as dangerous in the extreme and wholly unwarranted by the Constitution. His speech was a careful review of the constitutional aspects of the matter and a scathing rebuke to those who were seeking to effect a change for selfish purposes.

In the summer of 1876 it became known to General Leavenworth that his constituents desired to unanimously renominate him, but his increasing years and the great burden of the diversified interests that constantly called for his time and oversight impelled him to write a letter declining a renomination, of which the following is a copy :

WASHINGTON, D. C., July 1st, 1876.

To the Republican Electors of the Twenty-fifth Congressional District :

Gentlemen :—The time is now rapidly drawing near when you will again be called upon to select a candidate for the position which I now occupy. It is, therefore, proper that I should announce to you, as I now do, a decision of many months' standing—that I am not a candidate for the honor of a renomination. It has been an immemorial custom with each of the political parties to renominate members of Congress who have satisfactorily performed their duties. There has been no departure from this rule in the Twenty-fifth District during the last fifty years, if at any time, and probably would not be in the present instance. I am by no means insensible to the honor which it was your pleasure two years since, to bestow upon me, nor to that of the various important positions which have been conferred upon me during the last fifty years. For all these manifestations of kindness and confidence of the public, I must ever carry in my bosom feelings of the warmest gratitude. It may, therefore, be a matter of surprise to many of my friends that I should decline a renomination, and they may possibly feel desirous to know the reasons for so unusual a step.

It is well known to all my intimate friends, that I was reluctant to become a candidate for the nomination in 1874, and that I finally consented to do so at the urgent solicitation of the leading gentlemen of the Republican party in the district.

The same reasons which then influenced me still continue, and with undiminished force. The various responsible positions which I hold in the city and in the State, demand all my time, and the duty which I owe to those interested in the subjects committed to my care forbids that I should further neglect them. My duty requires me to relinquish those positions, or to relinquish the office which I now hold. This seems to me a sufficient reason for the course I now pursue, and here I might rest. But there are others not less potent,

At my time of life, I can not reasonably hope to enjoy many more years devoted to active and laborious duties. Those years, if allowed to me by an indulgent Providence, I desire to give to other and different pursuits. I am fully persuaded that I can be more useful at Syracuse than at Washington. I have in my mind desirable objects to be accomplished there, and they may be within my power. I am doing little here for the benefit of my constituents or the great public. Of the three committees on which I have been placed, not one of them during the last seven months has reported a bill, or done anything but "investigate." The investigations have disclosed nothing worth the paper which we have used in making them, unless, possibly, in one case of no public interest, and which was made at the suggestion of a Republican member. But all of them have been expensive and laborious, consuming much of our valuable time and drawing witnesses from remote parts of the Union, greatly to their inconvenience and at a heavy expense. I am not willing to waste more years in matters so unimportant and of so little value to my constituents, or the public, or myself.

There is also another reason which is quite as potent with me as the foregoing. I could under the most favorable circumstances hope to remain here but four years. This brief period of Congressional life scarcely suffices to educate a member for the duties he is called upon to perform. The great business of the House is always in the hands of the older members. They are the only persons who are fully advised in regard to most of the matters presented for our consideration. Most of the subjects presented, come before the House in some form each year. Old members become familiar with all the details, and it would be sheer impertinence for a new member to offer advice when surrounded by a large number of able members of large experience, each of whom is more competent to advise the House than himself. The House must first *know* a member—his integrity, his capacity, his fitness to advise on the great and intricate subjects committed to their care. The confidence of the House can be won only by slow degrees. Any attempt to force it will prove a failure, and one ordinarily fatal. Four years even would give a member but a partial education. Were I to remain so long, I should then *begin* to be useful, to be able to do something for my constituents and the country, and become more and more useful each year thereafter. I think it would not be extravagant to say that a single

34

member from the State of Massachusetts has had more influence on the legislation of this country for the last fifteen years, than the *entire* thirty-three members from the State of New York. It is most humiliating to visit the Capitol and witness our insignificance. Not that we lack talent, or education, or knowledge of various and important kinds, but we have not that particular branch of knowledge that can only be acquired on the floor of the House, but which is absolutely indispensable to any extended usefulness there. Other States are wiser. States with not a quarter of our number of members, have ten times our influence, and will continue to have, until we bring to the discharge of our political duties the same sagacity and wisdom which we so abundantly possess and make use of in our private affairs. This is our great, pressing, and paramount want.

Why have the Republican party of the Union just now honored the State of New York by selecting one of our fellow citizens for the second position of dignity and honor in this nation of fifty millions of people? Only because the Republican electors of the Nineteenth District have had the wisdom *five times* to select the Hon. Wm. A. Wheeler for the distinguished position which he now occupies. These ten years have made him well known in every State of this Union, his strong, vigorous common sense, his entire devotion to his duties and to the public good, his great abilities, his unimpeachable integrity, and his broad and comprehensive knowledge of our public affairs and of the country's wants. When the electors in other districts shall imitate the wisdom of those of the Nineteenth, and only then, shall we perform the duty that we owe to the country and to ourselves. Then, and only then, when we visit the proud capital of this great Nation, shall we have occasion to feel a just pride in the position which our State occupies in the Legislature of this Union. Whether that auspicious day shall ever come ; whether we shall in the future, as in the past, condemn ourselves to an ignominious and contemptible mediocrity, or rise to a position of honor and dignity and power worthy of our great State and of its position in the Union, depends as much upon the gentlemen whom I now address, as upon those of any other district in the State. I express myself upon this subject with perfect freedom, because, at my time of life, I cannot be suspected, even, of having any thought of myself in the above remark.

For these reasons, thus freely and frankly expressed, I must decline to be a candidate for renomination and will close this communication by expressing the hope that you will find in my successor a gentleman in all things fitted to adorn and dignify the office which I now hold, far better than I have been able to do, and that when such an one is found, you will permit no warring, intrusing politicians to deprive you of his valuable services, but will retain him in his position while he is willing to hold it and give to the country the great benefit of his large experience, his varied knowledge and the influence which he will necessarily acquire.   ELIAS W. LEAVENWORTH

General Leavenworth now found himself free from public office, strictly speaking, yet the incumbent of so many positions of trust in civil life that his time was still greatly occupied. He still retained the office of president of the Syracuse Savings Bank, which he held until 1883, when he tendered his resignation ; was president of the Syracuse Water Works Company, a position he had held since 1864 ; president of the Syracuse Gas Light Company, to which he was elected in 1872, though he had performed the duties of the office for fifteen years previous ; president of Oakwood Cemetery ; Regent of the University ; and a trustee of half a score of prominent institutions and associations, most of which positions he had held for many years and continued to occupy until his death. But in comparison with former years he was freed from arduous tasks and active labor. He felt that he could give more time to the pleasures of home and its social connections, to travel within the limits of his country, and to the completion and arrangement of his affairs preparatory to the great change that he realized could not be far in the future. His health, as far as related to organic disease, remained uniformly good and it was his pride and comfort that at eighty years of age he " felt none of the aches and pains of old age." The failure of his powers was gradual and natural, confining him to his bed for a few weeks at the close of his life, and on the 25th of November, 1887, he quietly passed to another life, his spirit serene and sustained by a trust in the mercy of his Creator and in an eternity of peace.

General Leavenworth was twice married; first on the 21st of June, 1833, to Mary Elizabeth Forman, daughter of Joshua Forman. Judge Forman has been accorded the honor of having been the founder of Syracuse. He was born in Duchess County, N. Y., September 6th, 1777, and graduated from Union College, after which he studied law in Philadelphia and New York. At the completion of his studies, he married Margaret Alexander, daughter of Boyd Alexander, M. P. for Glasgow, Scotland. In the spring of 1800 he removed to Onondaga Hollow. Here he soon acquired a large legal practice and in 1807 was elected to the Assembly, chiefly because of his ardent support of the Erie Canal scheme. From that time until the completion of the canal in 1825, he was, perhaps, more prominently instrumental in advancing its progress than any other man. In 1819, he took up his residence in Syracuse, prophecying against the opinion of all his friends, that a great city would arise where there was little else than forest and swamp. During the succeeding seven years he not only contributed more than any other person in laying sound and solid the foundation of the now thriving city, but also filled several public stations with marked ability. In 1829-30, Judge Forman removed to North Carolina, where he died on the 4th of August, 1848, and his remains now rest in beautiful Oakwood.

His daughter, (Mrs. Leavenworth) inherited many of the traits of character of her distinguished father, which fitted her in a peculiar degree for the companionship of such a man as General Leavenworth. During his long public career she was his constant companion and shared alike his struggles and triumphs. She died at the family residence in Syracuse on the 18th of April, 1880.

On the 12th of November, 1881, General Leavenworth was married to Mrs. Harriet Townley Ball, of Bergen, N. J., who survives him.

In the comments of prominent newspapers, his colleagues in the Board of Regents, and of the various representatives of the institutions with which he was intimately connected, a still fuller estimate of the character and great usefulness of General Leavenworth's life may be formed.

BURIAL SERVICE.

THE Burial Service of General Leavenworth was held in the afternoon of November 28th, 1887. The service began at the Leavenworth residence, on James street, at 1:30 o'clock; it was simple in character and attended by the family and nearest friends. Prayer was offered by the Rev. Dr. Spalding, after which the casket was borne to the hearse, followed by these gentlemen as pall bearers: George F. Comstock, Charles Andrews, Alfred A. Howlett, Wm. Brown Smith, Edward B. Judson, Nathan F. Graves, Daniel P. Wood, Andrew D. White, Carroll E. Smith, Robert G. Wynkoop, J. B. Moore, and Henry L. Duguid. In the funeral concourse were delegations from all the various organizations with which the deceased had been connected, the Chancellor of the Board of Regents, State Geologist James Hall, and a great number of private citizens. Arrived at the First Presbyterian church, the casket was borne into the enclosure by employees of one of the institutions with which the deceased had been identified, and placed upon a catafalque strewn with flowers, which stood in front of the pulpit. The choir then sang the beautiful hymn, "Like as a Father Pitieth his own Children," following which, prayer was offered by Rev. Dr. Codding

ton. A selection from Scripture was then read by Rev. Dr.
Spalding, at the close of which Rev. Dr. Coddington delivered
the following tribute to the deceased :

We are this day, dear friends, called to carry to burial the mortal remains of one
who has been, perhaps, the most conspicuous personage in the history of Syracuse.
The strength of this statement is, moreover, much emphasized by the fact that our city,
both in its earlier and in its later days, has been blessed with not a few whose great
eminence has been recognized far beyond its limits. Elias Warner Leavenworth goes
to the judgment day with vastly larger responsibilities to answer for than the great
majority of his fellow men. Providence endowed him with a magnificent natural
equipment, and the people gave to him the grandest opportunities for the beneficent
use of his powers. Coming to this city shortly after his admission to the bar in 1827,
he had completed sixty years of continuous professional and public life in this community. That alone is a privilege and a source of power accorded to but few individuals
in a generation, while, on the other hand, it is a severer test of personal character than
the vast majority of our mobile American people are ever subjected to. From the
year 1837, in which Mr. Leavenworth was elected a Trustee of the village, for the
major portion of a half century, he was actively engaged in public affairs, his fellow
citizens honoring his talent and his official integrity by repeated elevations to positions
of trust in city, county, State and national affairs. The records tell us that in 1838,
'39, and '40 he was made President of the village; in 1839 and '40 he served as Supervisor in the town of Salina ; in 1849 he was chosen Mayor of the city of Syracuse,
and again ten years later elected to the same office ; twice was he sent to represent
his fellow townsmen in the Legislature of the State ; in 1853 he was elected Secretary
of State ; in 1860 he was appointed one of the Board of Quarantine Commissioners
and served as President of that Board ; while as late as the year 1874, at the ripe age
of seventy, when most men would be both disinclined and, by the infirmities of age, to
a large extent incapacitated, to assume the severe labors and responsibilities of public
service, Mr. Leavenworth was again called forth by his fellow-citizens, this time elect-
ing him to a seat in the National Congress. Here he at once took rank among the
leaders of the House, serving with his usual assiduity and efficiency for a single term,
after which he positively declined a renomination. At these various posts of power
Mr. Leavenworth was able to leave a positive impress not only on the current social,
civil, political and charitable interests of his generation, but also to leave monumental
evidences of his best thought in the very structure of the city and State governments.

As late as 1872 he was appointed by the Governor and Senate of this State one of the thirty-two Commissioners to revise the Constitution of the State, and it is safe to say from the records of debate in that distinguished body, that none brought to its deliberations a broader understanding of the subject in hand, and none exerted a profounder influence upon its action. Under his official direction as Secretary of State, the census of 1855 was taken, the Capitol enlarged, the State Hall at Albany rebuilt, the publication of the Natural History of the State vigorously carried on, and the present supervision of State and local charitable institutions established. To his sagacity, also, we are to attribute the legislation creating a State Board of Assessors, and providing for the equalization of State taxes. In 1865 he served as President of the Board which placed at Batavia the institution for the blind, while it was chiefly through his influence that the State Asylum for Idiots was located here.

Such a brief review of some of the more important public offices held by the departed during his lifetime, must impress us with the fact that General Leavenworth was eminently a man of affairs. In these numerous and varied positions of responsibility he clearly evinced capacities and character qualifying him for the highest public trust, either at home or abroad, within the gift of the people. There is not a court in Europe which he would not have adorned in the service of his country.

A signal evidence of the largeness of the man is to be noticed in two facts of his history. The first was his capacity to impress himself on other men, men of the highest station and intelligence. Three different times was he taken from private life and appointed by the Governor of the State to the management of important and delicate public interests, and once was he thus called by the President of the United States, President Lincoln, in the year 1861, nominating and the Senate of the United States confirming him, as a Commissioner to adjust claims against New Granada. The second feature of his public history, evidencing his born leadership, is the remarkable fact that he was so generally chosen as president of the commissions, conventions, and other organizations of which, from time to time, he was a member. Yet, while a man of affairs, taking broad and general views of national policy, and in his plans even for city improvement, looking into the far future, he was also singularly accurate in matters of detail and of much narrower compass. Mr. Leavenworth had somewhat the instincts of the ancient scribe. The chronicles of family and town, of church and state, were all alike very sacred in his esteem. This has manifested itself in the genealogy of the family, so laboriously and excellently accomplished under his supervision, his unfaltering interest in the landmarks of local history, his prosecution of the work of publishing the Natural History of New York, while Secretary of State, and his successful effort while in the Legislature to secure the purchase by the State of Washington's headquarters at Newburg, and an appropriation for its continued preservation. His capacity to grasp a multitude of details and his very accurate memory of names and dates, a faculty continuing with unwonted power up to the last day of life, conspired with his love of family and country to make the study of history with him an increasing delight.

Standing by the bier of our departed friend and fellow-townsman this hour, we may well ask what lessons has that long and eminent public life for us who tarry yet a few days on the earth? To what may we attribute General Leavenworth's success in life? First, we would say to his industry, unremitting from his earliest studies of the law to his latest laboring day. Mr. Leavenworth was no idler in the field. Those who in his earlier years were intimately associated with him, as well as those who worked side by side with him in his later public life, all bear this unvarying testimony to his untiring industry. Great talent he undoubtedly possessed, but it was great talent utilized and enlarged by unceasing work. Such industry, however, was only possible to one who, at the beginning of his career, had been endowed with a sound body and had preserved it from organic disease up to the age of eighty-four by an abstemious mode of life. That on Friday morning last the dissolution of soul and body should come without a groan or the slightest contortion of a muscle, and that during all these weeks of decline not a pain should be experienced, argues that Mr. Leavenworth, from the beginning to the end, possessed a splendid bodily organism with which to do life's work. Since his decease we have been informed from sources which we deem entirely credible, that he never knew the taste of either whisky or tobacco, a most singular fact to be recorded of one who has been in American public life for more than half a century. A third prominent feature was to be found in his rigorous system. He knew where to find things, because he had a place for each and each in its place. This was as characteristic of his mental inventory as of the articles in his office desk. His precision of statement was only indicative of the clear order of his thought. General Leavenworth had a grasp and command of detail possessed by few men. We attribute this largely to his patience in labor, even to plodding, and to his rigorous system carried into every hour and into the least matters, even of domestic management. Above all, we may add, as the secret of his promotion, his proven integrity and efficiency in the performance of public duties committed to him. To-day no taint or corruption clouds the long continued official service of this man.

And, withal, General Leavenworth was a man of the people. Gifted with a commanding presence, his erect and graceful figure and his features of classical cast and strongly marked, made him a conspicuous center in any assemblage. Courtly in manners, but not statuesque, he commanded attention from the highest, while yet the hum-

44

blest approached him without fear. The courtesy of his nature, mindful of the least things, was a rare virtue needing to be much cultivated in our loud and brusque American society.

You will pardon me as I now, for the last time, stand in the presence of this venerable form, if I feel constrained to bring my little tribute of gratitude to the kindly spirit of the departed. Well do I remember seventeen years ago coming into this city, young and a stranger, with what courtesy and many unmerited attentions Mr. Leavenworth made me at home by his own fireside. During all the intervening years such kindness has been experienced in more ways than it would be proper for me to mention in this presence. They ceased only with that solemn hour, when, a few days ago, we were permitted to bow at the bedside of the dying, and there unite in prayer to God for forgiveness of sin, and commit the departing spirit to the mercy of God, through our Lord Jesus Christ.

After the singing of the beautiful hymn, "Thine Earthly Sabbaths," Rev. Dr. Spalding paid the following tribute to the deceased :

The picture which I have in my mind is that of a well-born, well-bred youth who, having received the culture which New England institutions and influences could give to him, came to this place sixty years ago this very month to begin his struggle for success. That large foresight which has signally characterized him at many a point in his brilliant career must have asserted itself at the beginning, enabling him to see beyond the poor, scanty settlement and the low, swampy site, the possibilities of a vigorous, beautiful city with its prosperous industries and its luxurious homes. With the ambition and energy which belong to youth, and with the sagacity and calculation which so often await our maturer years, this young lawyer entered at once upon a course of unusual good fortune. Rarely has there been a man who won for himself so many civic honors, so many offices of public trust, so large and continuous a material prosperity.

In reviewing this life, which has thus been so conspicuously passed before the eyes of successive generations, there is one feature of it most prominent of all, and well worthy of our contemplation.

We can easily picture to ourselves this young man of sixty years ago, keen-eyed, attractive in person and manners, energetic and yet methodical, so fully equipped for the struggle for fortune—we can easily picture him, or another like him, growing up with the growth of the community, eager to absorb unto himself a full share of its prosperity, engrossed wholly in building up a splendid success for himself alone. For-

45

tune is so won, success is so achieved by this intense, persistent application of all one's powers to the one object. But there is a nobler spirit than this, a larger success than this. There is such a thing as a strong, brilliant man plying with steadiness of purpose the conditions of his personal advantages, and winning his own individual triumphs, and yet, at the same time, with no less activity and wisdom, working for the general good of his community, contributing of his foresight and his culture for the increased intelligence, prosperousness and beauty of the town or city in which he lives.

To a very marked degree this has been an element in the career and fortune of him who lies before us to-day. Just as soon as Mr. Leavenworth had established his law firm and had opened his office to his clients, just so soon he began to work and plan for the enlargement and ornamentation of the village of Syracuse. His vision was broader than its broadest growth. He foresaw a great inland city, which would stretch through these valleys and crown the surrounding hills. He anticipated and hastened its wide expansion by a large system of conveniences and adornments which his vigorous, persistent will and his consummate taste were ever executing. For these three score of years, while busy in amassing his own fortune and gathering in his almost boundless official honors, and discharging with utmost diligence and fidelity all his public trusts, State and municipal, he has been equally busy in laying out and widening streets, opening parks, planting trees—making every highway and square of the city to respond to his most exquisite sense of the becoming and the beautiful.

There are those who will carry to their graves the picture of an old man, graceful in form and manners, alert in every movement, superintending the placing of tree after tree whose spreading verdure and shade make up the chief glory of our finest streets. Sometimes in the drouth of summer, it has been his own hands that have watered their parched roots, and so preserved for generations the grateful coolness of these umbrageous walks. They will long stand as living monuments, their every leaf as they rustle in the summer's breeze, telling to every passer-by of the beneficence and munificent public spirit of General Leavenworth. We all have a great pride in this city. Strangers who visit us extol its beauty. Let us not forget the hand that, during all this formative period, has shaped its loveliness.

During these years there have been springing up great banking institutions whose chief blessings have fallen upon the laboring classes. It was the ever restless brain of this man which projected the first of these savings banks. He knew that such institutions are indispensable to a growing city, opening up new resources of wealth to the wealthy, but more than this, securing comfort and independence to the vast number who without these would become wasteful and impoverished. He no more planted these trees for his exclusive benefit than he reared these banks for his own enrichment. The same public spirit, the same noble sense of the common weal ruled in both actions. We rejoice to-day in the prosperity of these great moneyed institutions. Other cities acknowledge their superior excellence. Let us not forget whose far-sighted enterprise and generous method led the way to their establishment.

Along these streets, upon many a crowning site, there are homes for the aged and asylums and hospitals for the unfortunate. They attest to the Christian kindness, to the humane compassion of the city's inhabitants. They are among our chief glories. Let us not forget that the very existence of some of them is owing to the generosity and the personal guardianship of him whom we mourn to-day.

For months after I came to this city I wondered, as I looked up at the grand, massive spire of this church, and marked the fine proportions of wall and buttress, and walking within, gazed with such perfect satisfaction at its stately columns, its waving arches, and its far-off embracing roof, every part of the noble edifice meeting my sense of beauty and filling my soul with worship. I for a long time wondered how it could be that so far back in the history of this city, when its wealth must have been small, and its taste crude, such a temple of fitness and beauty could have been erected. It detracts nothing from the full meed of praise which even to-day we would give to those other noble men, who forty years ago were associated with General Leavenworth in planning the new church, to say that it was his far-sighted wisdom, and his refined æsthetic nature and his overmastering will that determined the fair and stately forms that arise around us here to-day. His own dream of beauty at last crystalized into this faultless structure which age has touched only to make it more beautiful. This church through these many years, has been the pride of this man's heart. He served it long and well. The last smile that broke upon his face as I stood with him in the presence of death, was evoked by my announcement to him that that very day the last burden of debt was raised from it, and it was left free to go on its way rejoicing. He loved this church. As long as its spire and its arches point upward, and congregations crowd its walls, it will stand a monument of the cultured taste, the far-reaching, sagacious perception and public spirit of this band of men who generously accepted his leadership.

General Leavenworth during these two last years of his extreme age, the only time I have ever known him, has been exhibiting, to my surprise and admiration, the same large, broad view of affairs, the same onward looking, the same wondrous energy that characterized him so grandly in the days of his youthful fervor, and in the years of his manhood's devotion. He has given largely and inspired others to give largely for the extension of Presbyterianism in this city, so that since he passed the line of his four

47

score years of life, two commodious and elegant churches have arisen to gather worshipers within their walls. And already, even before the sound of the hammer had ceased to ring within the last of these churches, he was busy in projecting another to meet the growing religious wants of the city.

And now, you, who have for so many years been associated with this man in his busy work, applauding his wisdom and fruitful activities, enjoying with us the results of his affluent taste and creative culture, with reverent step will bear him to his last resting place. But even there, at his and your own journey's end, you will behold on every side in that city of the dead the same evidences of his far-reaching vision, ceaseless industry and transforming grace. So many years ago, nearly thirty, General Leavenworth was leading the way for the purchase of this tract of land, which nature, as if for this special purpose, through the slow ages, had been molding into fullest shape. During all these years since the artist's taste and the deft hand of Mr. Leavenworth have been steadily at work, until Oakwood cemetery has become a place of all others the most beautiful as the sleeping place of our dead. There you will with tender hands lay him down amidst the scenes of quietude and loveliness which his genius has evoked.

For weeks past, this man who has conquered so much in life, has been lying face to face with Him who is the conqueror of us all. With open eyes he has been peering into the grave and into the eternity beyond. I have beheld his great serenity, his unruffled peace. In humble tones he spoke, to the last, of his defects and faults. With trustful soul he cast himself where we must all find our only safe rest, upon the abounding mercies of our God in Jesus Christ.

The service closed with a benediction pronounced by Rev. Dr. Spalding.

The interment was made on the beautiful spot which was selected by the deceased at the time of the dedication of the cemetery.

> " And when the stream
> Which overflowed the soul was passed away,
> A consciousness remained that it had left,
> Deposited upon the silent shore
> Of memory, images and precious thoughts
> That shall not die, and cannot be destroyed."

TRIBUTES.

ALTHOUGH General Leavenworth reached a ripe old age and his earthly labor may be said to have been well done, yet his death caused a feeling of sadness throughout the State and even beyond its boundaries, while in the city of Syracuse the evidence of sorrow was universal. It found expression in many ways, and it is appropriate that the more public tributes offered to his worth while living and to his memory when dead shall find a place in these few pages.

A Special meeting of the Common Council of Syracuse was called to take action on the death of General Leavenworth at which a Committee was appointed who reported the following, which was unanimously adopted :

Elias Warner Leavenworth died at his late residence in the city of Syracuse, November 24th, 1887, having nearly completed the 84th year of his age.

Upon the completion of his education at Yale college and the Litchfield law institution, twenty years before Syracuse became a city, he identified his life and his interests with the life and interests of this community. In the thirty-fourth year of his age he became a trustee of the village and several years thereafter served it in the capacity of President of the Board of Trustees. He was the second Mayor of the city of Syracuse, and again in 1859 occupied that honorable and responsible position.

During the earlier years of his residence here he established a large and lucrative law practice. Two years he represented his town in the Board of Supervisors. Twice he was elected Member of Assembly. In 1853 he was elected Secretary of State, and thereafter rendered important public services for the State at large. He served as President of the first Board of Quarantine Commissioners. For more than twenty-five years he served as a Regent of the State University. For many years as a Trustee of the State Idiot Asylum, the location of which in this city was largely due to his efforts. During his young manhood he took active interest in the organization and development of the State militia service, in which he rose to the rank of brigadier-general.

In 1872 he was appointed one of the thirty-two Commissioners to revise the Constitution of this State. He served one term as Representative of this district in Congress, and declined a renomination. As President of the Commission to establish a sewerage system he rendered important service to the city. For many years he served as President of the Syracuse Water Company, Syracuse Gas Works, Oakwood Cemetery Association, and of the Syracuse Savings Bank. He also rendered important service as trustee of many of our charitable institutions.

During his first term as Mayor, the Syracuse Water Works Company and the Syracuse Savings Institution were organized and incorporated. During that term was enacted the law authorizing the reclamation and improvement of a tract of low and marshy land bordering upon Onondaga creek, which was thereby restored to healthfulness and rendered an important acquisition to the city. During his second term as Mayor the various independent fire companies theretofore existing were consolidated and incorporated into the "Fire Department of the City of Syracuse." Many other public services were rendered by him during these sixty years of ceaseless activity.

More than of any other one man it may be truthfully said that the development of the little village community of sixty years ago, into the vigorous and progressive municipality, embracing the manifold institutions and enterprises of to-day, is the product of his brain and of his enterprise.

The list of citizens who, at an early date, contributed largely to the development and improvement of this community includes such names as Forman, Burnet, Noxon, Lawrence, Baldwin, Smith, Granger, Forbes, Burt, Teall, and Van Buren. All of these we remember with gratitude. To-day we add another name to the roll of our honored dead. With reverent hearts we bow before the shrine of our Past, made earnest, made strong, made progressive by the memory of those names that are written in the marble.

To no one of these names will the mind oftener recur than to his we mourn to-day, as an exponent of the sagacity, probity, and energy of the pioneers who organized, nurtured and firmly established this beautiful and prosperous city.

With larger opportunities and improved facilities, it will be well if the present generation shall do its work upon the superstructure as they did theirs upon the foundations.

RESOLVED, That as we bow submissive to the divine decree, we desire to testify in behalf of the city of Syracuse, our acknowledgement of the important services to this community in the life just closed. That we tender to the family of the deceased our respectful sympathy in their bereavement. That the clerk be directed to enter this testimonial upon the official records of the city. That as a further testimony of respect we will attend the funeral in a body.

52

A meeting of the Board of Trustees of the Syracuse Savings Bank was held on the 29th of November, 1887, at which the following resolutions were adopted :

RESOLVED, That the trustees have heard with profound sorrow of the death of Elias W. Leavenworth, the former president of this bank. He was a trustee from the organization of the bank, for more than a quarter of a century its president, and continued from year to year until increasing years led him to resign the office and seek repose from the more active duties of life.

That during the long time he occupied the position of president he discharged all the duties of the office with distinguished ability. He was always faithful and vigilant in the discharge of his duties and always maintained the most exalted integrity. During his administration the bank grew from a very small beginning to be one of the strong and established institutions of the country.

That for more than half a century he has been identified with Syracuse and with all its best interests. He was a trustee of the village and for several years its president, and was twice the mayor of the city, and has held many offices of trust and importance, and has always exercised an influence for good in every position that he has held. He was positive, vigorous and courageous, and never shrank from any duty. He was a friend of every good cause, and dealt out with a liberal hand to any object of charity and to all works of public beneficence. He had a distinguished ancestry and added greatly to the renown of the town.

He was a member of the First Presbyterian church. He reached a great age and has been brought gradually to his end. He was perfectly resigned and entered into rest in a good old age in his own beautiful house, surrounded by those whom he loved, with all the consolations of the religion that he professed.

RESOLVED, That we will, as a body, attend the religious services of his funeral, and that we tender a copy of these resolutions to his family as a feeble expression of our sympathy and regard, and that these resolutions be published in the journals of the city.

At a meeting of the Board of Trustees of the First Presbyterian Society of Syracuse, of which General Leavenworth was for many years a member and officer, held on the 26th of November, 1887, the following memorial and resolutions were unanimously adopted :

Elias W. Leavenworth died at his late residence in the city of Syracuse, November 24th, 1887. His connection with this society covers almost the entire period of its corporate existence. For nearly or quite fifty years he has been a member of this board, and almost the same length of time he has been its clerk. Within the period during which the oldest of us has been associated with this society there has been no time that he failed to occupy a position of commanding influence in its affairs. During almost the entire history of the society his active mind and liberal hand and intelligent, far-sighted purpose have to a large extent made its history. During the fifty years past many a large enterprise has been undertaken and accomplished, and in all of these he was a leader. Identified with the early days of the village of Syracuse, his keen vision foresaw the development of our growth and resources, and from those early days his determined purpose to build up a religious society commensurate in its capacity and undertakings with the future growth of the town has been uniformly manifest. Public-spirited and liberal-handed, vigilant, energetic and persistent, he has done more than any one now living to secure the high vantage ground now occupied by this church. To the very last his sympathies and energies were largely enlisted in our behalf. His death so swiftly following that of his life-long friend and co-worker, our late associate, Harmon W. Van Buren, removes almost, if not quite, the last survivor of the first period of our church history. The passing away of these, who by their labors secured for us the blessed heritage we now enjoy, admonishes us not only of the mortality of man, but of his duty to work while the day lasts. By their departure we enter into the solemn obligation to defend and perpetuate in all its capacity for usefulness the noble society which they founded, nurtured and firmly established.

RESOLVED, That we mourn the death of Elias W. Leavenworth as the removal of one with a sagacity so far-sighted, a personality and history so filled with useful power, always possessed of a purpose so large-minded and liberal-spirited that we feel it impossible to fill his place.

That the clerk be directed to inscribe this tribute to his memory upon the records of the society and express to his family our heartfelt sympathy in their bereavement.

That we attend the funeral of our associate in a body.

At a meeting of the directors of the Gas Light Company, held at its office in Syracuse on Saturday, November 26, 1887, it was resolved, that it is a rare occurrence in a community so young as the city of our home, for the demise of one for sixty years a resident within its borders—honored and respected, entering in the quest of objects that might minister to its general welfare, and giving freely of his time and abilities, in their inception, prosecution and maintenance, and in which he has drawn to himself the respect and esteem of his fellow citizens.

General Leavenworth came into the councils of the Gas Light company in the fourth year of its existence and was, at his decease, its third president, succeeding the late James Lynch, who was the successor of Moses D. Burnet, its first president. As such he has been uniformly present at its meetings, active in the promotion of its interests, uniformly courteous and genial in his intercourse with his fellow directors.

In the close by death of this long period of mutual labors, we record a distinct recognition of his activeness and zeal in its management and our deep regrets at its termination, and we tender his family our warmest sympathy in their bereavement.

RESOLVED, That the directors and officers of this company will attend his funeral in a body.

At a meeting of the trustees of Oakwood held on Saturday, November 26, 1887, the following resolutions were adopted :

RESOLVED, That we mourn the loss of our president, Elias W. Leavenworth, and tender to his family and friends our condolences in deep sympathy with their and our great loss.

RESOLVED, That the trustees of Oakwood will attend his funeral in a body.

RESOLVED, That the following memorial, adopted and spread upon our minutes, shall be presented to his family by our secretary:

IN MEMORIAM.

The remains of our venerable president, Elias W. Leavenworth, will soon be laid to rest in the beautiful cemetery over the affairs of which he has long and ably presided. For several years before the organization of Oakwood his attention was directed towards the grounds selected in 1859. The officers first elected were: E. W. Leavenworth, president; A. C. Powell, vice-president; Hamilton White, treasurer; and Allen Munroe, secretary; all now departed, our worthy chief the last to lay aside the office which he had continuously and honorably held from the beginning. In the ever-recurring cycles of time and the ever-changing seasons, twenty-nine times have the flowers withered and the leaves fallen since our beloved president took charge of the laying out and beautifying the lands of Oakwood. The results of his labors are too well known and appreciated to need recapitulation.

Thou faithful servant, the dignified and courteous gentleman, rest in peace! The winds of November, now passing mournfully through the leafless branches, will be forgotten when the soft air of spring shall clothe in verdure the hill-sides and trees of our beautiful cemetery, and with every blade of grass and every bursting bud and opening flower thy memory will remain with ever-pleasant thoughts.

The following tribute of respect and affection was proposed and adopted by the Board of Counselors of the Syracuse Home Association:

The Syracuse Home Association and Board of Managers are called upon to-day to record the departure from this life of the oldest member of the Board of Counselors.

We find that General E. W. Leavenworth became a member of the Board at the seventh annual meeting in 1859. In 1860, he was made secretary of the Board and retained that position until his death. His name is therefore conspicuous through the greater part of the history of the association.

He bore an active part in all the duties of that Board and we cannot know how much we are indebted to his wisdom in council for the present prosperous condition of the Association. He was one of the early and regular contributors to its funds; was one of the building committee for erection of the Home, and we are indebted to him for the original furnishing of one of the rooms. We always expected to see him at the annual meeting and on New Year's day.

He and his contemporaries have all passed away and their places are now filled by others who, we trust, will be as firm and true to the interests of the Association as they were. We shall miss him who so long filled a prominent and responsible position, and while we feel that he had lived to see more than all the good of life, yet we know he will be greatly missed in his home, and we would tender our warmest sympathies to the several members of his family and pray that the consolation of the Gospel of our Lord and Saviour may be theirs in an especial measure at this time.

The following was adopted at a meeting of the Board of Directors of the Syracuse Water Company:

RESOLVED, That the following tribute to the memory of Gen. Elias W. Leavenworth be spread upon the minutes of this meeting of the Board of Directors of the Syracuse Water Company, and that a copy thereof be properly attested and sent to his family: It is but seldom that death gathers in men of such fruitful lives as was the life which General Leavenworth has just closed, one which distinguished him as a scholar, a business man and a gentleman. He was the city's foremost citizen, and its most enterprising, public-spirited, and energetic benefactor. In his professional life he earned honors; his business career was no less successful, and political preferment came to him of right. Genial in his social relations, his acquaintance was wide and among leading minds; generous and kindly toward all, all alike mourn his death, though he goes down to his grave with the golden sheaf of age upon his casket. He was the oldest member of this company, for many years its able president, and for half a century a most influential director; and in both capacities his ability and fidelity were never questioned, his keen foresight never doubted, and his almost unequaled energy never spent in vain. While we shall mourn the absence and miss the wise counsel of our friend and associate, we shall remember with pleasure and gratitude his most valuable services and the uniform courtesy and urbanity with which they were so faithfully performed. As the great oak is among the forest of oaks, so was General Leavenworth among men. As the great oak falls by reason of the lapse of time, so fell our friend—his duty done. We tender our heartfelt sympathy and offer condolence to the mourning family, and in token of the earnestness of our expressions we will attend the funeral in a body, and be it ordered that the office of the Water Company be closed on the afternoon of the funeral.

The trustees of the Onondaga Orphan Asylum met and adopted the following resolutions of respect to General Leavenworth, who was at his death the oldest member of their Board:

WHEREAS, We are once more called upon as a board of trustees of the Onondaga County Orphan Asylum, to bury from our number General E. W. Leavenworth, the oldest member of our board, both by reason of age and continuity of service in behalf of the asylum. For forty-one years has our departed friend and coassociate given us the benefit of his valuable services and judicious counsel. By more than ten years does his membership antedate that of any member of this board, and of those who were associated with him in the early history of the asylum as trustees, all have laid down their burden and gone to their reward.

RESOLVED, That in the death of General E. W. Leavenworth this board has lost one to whom it has looked for counsel; one who was deeply interested in the welfare and success of the asylum, and one who amid the cares and anxieties of business was ever ready and willing to give of his time and means to promote its interests.

We shall miss his genial presence and kindly greeting and wise counsel, while the orphans have lost a friend and benefactor. We tender to his bereaved and sorrowing family our heartfelt sympathy ; that we will attend his funeral in a body, and that this expression of our feelings be entered at large upon the minutes of our Board and a copy be sent to the family of our deceased friend and late associate.

The following memorial and resolutions were adopted at a meeting of the Onondaga Coarse Salt Association :

This Association is called to mourn the loss of one of its oldest members. A resident of this city for sixty years, has passed away in the fullness of his years and in the midst of a community where, in the vigor of his young manhood, his active and professional and business life commenced and where it is now closed. To mention the various duties that he has performed and the many public trusts that have been committed to his charge by his fellow citizens, would be to recite the history of the village and the city of Syracuse. He was proud of our growth and prosperity, and prophesied still greater increase for the future, and he inspired in others the sentiments that he so fondly cherished.

RESOLVED, That the death of Hon. E. W. Leavenworth leaves a void in this community and a loss that we cannot estimate, and now that his name has been added to the long list of early settlers that have passed away, may we, the survivors, strive to fill their places with equal usefulness and honor.

RESOLVED, That we herewith tender to the family and relatives our condolence and our sympathy.

RESOLVED, That as a further mark of our regard we will attend the funeral in a body from the First Presbyterian church this afternoon.

At the annual meeting of the Board of Regents of the University, held on the 12th of January, 1888, the Chancellor announced the death of General Leavenworth and paid a feeling and highly eulogistic tribute to the deceased, in which he said :

In this Board he was vigilant and sagacious, full of wise and generous suggestions. Of a masterful temperament, he was tenacious of his own views and he maintained them with great independence and ability, but his mind was open and hospitable to every form of progress, and he bore himself always with unfailing courtesy. To the last he was singularly alert and energetic, health unbroken, his interest untiring. In old age he was still young, and by his public activities and his personal character, his associates of this Board gratefully feel themselves cheered and stimulated. The State loses in him one of the men who make the strength of States, and his immediate community a citizen most worthy of emulation.

Regent Bostwick offered the following tribute to the memory of his deceased colleague:

MR. CHANCELLOR: There are but few men living to-day who have been so long and intimately connected with the various departments of our State government as was the late General Leavenworth. He was better informed on the legislative, political and educational history of the State than any man I have ever met. For more than forty years he has been the direct representative of the people, and whether as President of his village, Mayor of his city, in the State Legislature, Secretary of State, or Representative in Congress, his influence was felt in every position he occupied.

He was a man of broad views, and thoroughly practical in his ideas. General Leavenworth was always on the side of progress and good government. He possessed an intense State pride, and promoted many of the enterprises which have given glory and honor to the State. He was ever foremost in matters of education, as his record in the Board of Regents for more than a quarter of a century attests. He was generous and patriotic, and of him it may be truly said: "He loved his country and his fellow-man."

We shall miss his genial presence and wise counsels in this Board. He left the impress of his character upon the works he had in hand. His labors never ceased until his great heart ceased to pulsate. He died in the fullness of mental vigor, at an age beyond the allotted three score and ten. His life was full of good works, and his memory will be cherished for the many noble traits of character which were exemplified in his long and useful life.

The following eloquent tribute was then pronounced by Regent Watson:

MR. CHANCELLOR: After the very eloquent tribute to which we have listened this evening, I trust that it may not be considered unbecoming in me (representing with my distinguished colleague, ex-Senator Kernan, as I do, the city where Regent Leavenworth commenced the practice of his profession, and from which, on the suggestion of that eminent advocate of Utica, Joshua A. Spencer, he removed to Syracuse, his future home, where for sixty years he remained one of its most conspicuous citizens) to make a few brief remarks upon the life and character of our lamented associate.

The senior member of this Board, by his devoted attention to its interests, his never-failing attendance upon its meetings, and his uniform urbanity of manner, conjoined with many other eminent qualities of mind and heart, greatly endeared himself to all his associates.

Comparatively few, indeed, Mr. Chancellor, even among those who have had opportunity for the highest culture in their earlier years, are the men, eminent in business, politics, law or medicine, who, amid the hurry, the bustle and confusion, the ceaseless push and wear and tear of our modern life, resolutely and daily snatch a few brief moments from the rapidly fleeting hours to return to those studies which, in the language of the greatest of Roman orators, "are the ornament of prosperity, the comfort and refuge of adversity, and the solace and delight of old age." Such a man, however, was our lamented colleague.

Amid the engrossing cares and wearing anxieties of even the most active period of his busy political and professional life, he yet found time to make not infrequent excursions into the realms of literature and art and to gather thence those flowrets of culture and of taste, the sweet perfume of which will ever linger in the memory of those who were so fortunate as to have enjoyed his intimate acquaintance.

Mr. Chancellor, as well as in many other traits of character, he was a bright and shining exemplar for the younger men of his generation.

The white snow of mid-winter (fit emblem of the purity of character of him who sleeps beneath) rests gently upon his recent grave, in that beautiful cemetery of which he was the originator and the greatest benefactor, of the fair city of Central New York which was his home, and which his wonderful energy, his great business enterprise and untiring industry, his "affluent taste and creative culture" had done so much to enrich and to adorn ; and we may not inappropriately apply to our late associate the words inscribed upon the tomb of the great architect of St. Paul's Cathedral, Sir Christopher Wren, who, at the age of ninety (but six years older than our departed friend), was laid at rest in the crypt of his own beautiful church, "*Si monumentum requiris circumspice.*"

Bis vixit, qui bene, was the saying of a most distinguished moralist of antiquity. Tried by this test, how far prolonged and how fruitful in good works appear the more than fourscore years of our departed colleague.

Vice-Chancellor Curtis then delivered the following tribute to his deceased colleague :

Mr Chancellor : Our little circle, although always complete, is always changing. Time may creep on with petty pace from day to day, but it surely brings to-morrow, and to-morrow and to-morrow, with the only foot that never tires, and never reaches a bourne. It seems to me but yesterday that I was the youngest member of this Board, and now the death of Mr. Leavenworth leaves me in date of election, the senior member. In the French academy each newly elected member, upon taking his seat, delivers an eulogy of his predecessor, and it is but a fitting duty to which you summoned me in asking me to prepare a brief minute upon our late associate. But it is not a ceremony only ; it is an act of cordial friendship and high respect.

The distinguishing trait of Mr. Leavenworth seems to me to have been his public spirit. From his removal to Syracuse to his death, he was always conspicuous in its good works of every kind. His untiring energy, his quick intelligence, his warm sympathy and firmness and urbanity, were qualitities of the utmost service in the rapid growth of the city. There are certain characteristics which mark the English gentleman, and Tennyson, as you remember in the familiar lines, says of his friend, Arthur Hallam, that he

> " bore without abuse
> The grand old name of gentleman."

The poet does not define the word. He appeals to the universal consciousness of the English-speaking race. In the same way Mr. Leavenworth's peculiar qualities and interests and devotion were such as distinguished the American citizen. He was in no sense a servile flatterer of the mob, nor in any way a panderer to vulgar prejudice. He did not hold mere popularity to be the evidence of genuine patriotism or effective public service. The test of sincere Americanism is not deference to the views of others, It is the unquailing courage of your own opinions.

During the later years of his life in which I knew him, Mr. Leavenworth signally illustrated the difference between public service and political ambition. I do not mean, of course, that they are incompatible. Mr. Leavenworth had strong political convictions and warm party feeling. But his public interest and activity did not depend upon official position. As a private person he would have been a benificent force in any community. He belonged to that class of Americans who by their characters and abilities are necessarily public men. Their views are sought ; their counsels are heeded ; their integrity commands confidence ; their judgment molds local public opinion, and their practical sagacity directs public action.

How well we recall, Mr. Chancellor, his vigorous good sense in the deliberations of this Board, his wide intelligence, his sound discretion. That hale and hearty figure, all unbowed by the snowy years, rises before me as I speak and that kindly courtesy seems almost impatiently to deprecate my words of praise. I saw a letter from our friend during the summer, in which he said, " at eighty-four I feel none of the aches and pains of age." That tranquil citizen, persistent in good deeds, discredited Wordsworth's lines:

> " The good die first
> And those whose hearts are dry as summer's dust
> Burn to the socket."

But how nobly at the end he illustrated those other lines of Wordsworth :

> " But an old age serene and bright
> And lovely as a Lapland night
> Shall lead thee to thy grave."

The press of Syracuse, as well as generally throughout the State, published extended biographical sketches of General Leavenworth, the matter of which is embodied in preceding pages of this Memorial. In addition to the editorial expressions incorporated in such sketches, several prominent journals made separate editorial comment upon his long and useful life and the great public loss caused by his death. From those comments are selected the following brief extracts :

60

Yesterday the slow sinking away of General E. W. Leavenworth's bodily powers ended in death. The event removes from the city a long familiar figure and a mind active to the last in all its operations and sympathies. He had held important offices in the State, discharging each responsibility with energetic fidelity, and he had served the nation; but, when compelled by accumulated years to contract the circle of his activities, he continued to maintain important relations with the people of Syracuse and interest himself warmly in whatever interested them. The younger generation of Syracusans did not often think of him, probably, as one who had served the commonwealth in places of dignity, and had engaged in the conferences of the State's political chiefs. To them the old man who sank into his last sleep yesterday at the age of almost four score years and four, was an ancient landmark, one of the first citizens of the town in age, intelligence, wealth, social rank and public spirit. Moving among us with stateliness and courtliness, still bearing traces of his comely prime, he has long been the most prominent person connecting the Syracuse of to-day with the little village out of which it has risen. He has watched with keen pleasure every movement in its expansion, every undertaking for its adornment, and has been, himself, a leading contributor to its prosperity and beauty.

Elias W. Leavenworth identified himself most intimately full sixty years with this community, and the monuments of his intelligent zeal are visible on every hand. These pronounce a better eulogy than will be written or spoken, and they will arrest attention after the voice of praise is stilled, and the city which he saw with pride rise to new estates of dignity, shall have outstripped his fondest dreams of greatness.

Very closely interwoven with the history of Syracuse is the story of the life that, like a candle, flickered out yesterday in a stately James street mansion. Coming to Syracuse sixty years ago, fresh from Yale college and the Litchfield law school, General Leavenworth early took a deep interest in all that concerned the growth and prosperity of our then village—an interest which never waned during his long career as a citizen. Fifty years ago he was village Trustee and for several years thereafter the village President. Forty years ago, less two, he was Mayor of the city, and again thirty years ago, less two. Twenty-five years ago he was candidate for Congress before the Republican convention, which sat five days before it made a choice, the other candidates being Charles B. Sedgwick, Thomas T. Davis, and R. Holland Duell. The three Onondaga candidates, Sedgwick, Davis and Leavenworth, are now numbered with the dead. General Leavenworth's single term in Congress was an eventful period, and he occupied a conspicuous position in that body.

General Leavenworth's ideas in relation to city affairs were, as a rule, of an advanced order. He believed in broad streets, in shade trees, and especially in systematized improvements. He advocated for years the creation of a Board of Public Works, clothed with full supervision and authority over our streets, and particularly over the laying out of new streets and parks. Our narrow streets, often laid out regardless of system, gave him great distress. The city would have been vastly the gainer if it had followed General Leavenworth's wise suggestions. In his death the city loses one of its most public-spirited and far-sighted citizens, one who has made a deep impress on its history.

At the close of a lengthy sketch of General Leavenworth's life, the editor wrote: "No more active man has ever resided here, and his busy life has borne valuable results in many directions. While a person of infinite detail, yet he was naturally a strong executive and guided with intelligence and firmness. He habitually impressed his views upon those with whom he was associated, and most excellent judgment was shown in his practical methods of carrying them into execution. There were few public enterprises in this community, in the first half century of our city's existence, that he was not a foremost figure in shaping, and probably no more public spirited and useful citizen has ever resided in Syracuse.

The death of General E. W. Leavenworth removes one of the foremost citizens of Syracuse. He had been so long identified with the city's interests that his absence will be everywhere a source of sorrow and loss. He had rounded out a full measure of years, and had lived to see his struggling and straggling town become a large and prosperous city.

General E. W. Leavenworth, ex-Secretary of State, and ex-member of Congress, died in Syracuse this morning. He was born in Canaan, N. Y., December 20, 1803, graduated at Yale in the class of 1824, and came to Syracuse to live three years later, having in the meantime studied law with William Cullen Bryant, and at the Litchfield (Conn.) Law School. In 1841 he became Brigadier-General of the State militia; he was member of Assembly in 1850 and 1856, Secretary of State in 1854-5, and Mayor of Syracuse in 1849 and 1859, having also held prominent offices there before the city was incorporated.

Gen. Leavenworth was elected Secretary of State by the Whig party, and was very prominent and active in that office. The State Asylum for Idiots was located in Syracuse by his efforts. He presided over the Republican State Convention that sent a delegation of friends of William H. Seward to the National Republican Convention of 1860. In 1861 he was nominated by President Lincoln Commissioner to adjust claims against New Granada. Membership in the State Constitutional convention (1867), in two State Boundary Commissions, in Congress (1874-5), and for the last twenty-six years in the Board of Regents, indicate some of his other public services. With local business institutions he was also closely identified.

Elias Warner Leavenworth was born in Canaan, N. Y., December 20, 1803, but his early childhood was passed in Great Barrington, Mass., where he received an academic education. After a short time spent at Williams College he entered Yale, from which institution he was graduated in 1824. Subsequently he studied law, first with William Cullen Bryant, and later at the once famous law school at Litchfield, Conn. After being admitted to the bar in 1827, he settled in Syracuse and followed his profession until compelled by ill health to abandon it in 1850. Mr. Leavenworth first entered public life in 1835, when he was elected member of the Assembly. The following year he was made Brigadier-General in command of the State artillery. He was President of the village of Syracuse in 1839, 1840, 1841, 1846, and 1847, and its Mayor in 1849 and 1859. He was continually a member of the Assembly from 1850 to 1857, with the exception of two years' service in 1854 and 1855, as Secretary of State. He was a Regent of the State University, and so was unable to accept the office of Trustee for Hamilton College, to which he was elected in 1867. Five years later the college conferred upon him the degree of Doctor of Laws. Gen. Leavenworth held a number of minor offices under the State and United States government, and was one of the commissioners under the convention with New Granada. He was a member of the Forty-Fourth Congress from the Syracuse district.

LETTERS.

WHEN the news of the death of General Leavenworth came like a dark shadow into the homes of the innumerable friends of the family, and to the knowledge of his former official associates and his wide circle of acquaintances, there came to his remaining household, numberless personal missives of condolence and sympathy, all deeply expressive of the high appreciation in which the writers held their deceased friend. Most of these letters had an almost sacred personal and private character, intended only for the family circle. The few that follow, however, may properly be placed in these pages:

FROM WM. H. WATSON, UTICA, N. Y., REGENT OF THE STATE UNIVERSITY.

I was shocked and deeply grieved to hear of the death of General Leavenworth. The senior member of the Board of Regents, your distinguished husband, by his devoted attention to the interests of the Board, his never-failing attendance at its meetings, and his uniform urbanity of manner, conjoined with many other eminent qualities of mind and heart, had rendered himself greatly endeared to all his associates in that body.

Amid the engrossing cares and wearing anxieties of even the most active periods of his busy political and professional life, he yet found time to make not infrequent excursions into the realms of literature and art and to gather there those flowerets of culture and of taste, the sweet perfume of which will ever linger in the memory of those who were so fortunate as to enjoy his intimate acquaintance.

The many and varied public offices which he so acceptably filled, attest alike the versatility of his talents and the exalted estimation in which he was held by his fellow citizens of Syracuse, as well as by the people of the State.   *   *   *

FROM HENRY R. PIERSON, CHANCELLOR OF THE BOARD OF REGENTS.

When I received your telegram announcing the death of the dear old man to whom I owe so much and whose memory is embalmed in my heart, I thought of sending an immediate telegraphic answer of sympathy, and then decided to wait until I could write. I was not surprised. I was as well prepared as I could be when not confronted with death itself, for which there is no complete preparation; but now I am not surprised, and I beg to share in your sorrow, even a little. He was a noble man; so genial and so just; so thoughtful and so true; so faithful and so trusting; so dear a friend and so guileless. I loved the dear man, and I am so glad I knew him. He has added greatly to my pleasure and helped me to be a wiser and a better man. I sorrow with you, but he has left us a rich inheritance in a noble life.

FROM B. D. SILLIMAN, BROOKLYN, N. Y.

On returning to town this evening, I am met by the sad, sad telegram from Syracuse. I need not—I can not—tell you how deeply I sympathize with you in this great affliction—the death of my dear, constant friend from boyhood to our old age. But his has been a long, a good, a useful, a noble, a distinguished, and a very honored life, and his death peaceful and painless. What a grand career—what an enviable death! I should, were I able, be with you on Monday, but am hardly adequate to the journey. I shall, in heart, be among the mourners who will linger at his grave.

FROM E. A. DICKINSON, SECRETARY BOARD OF TRUSTEES OF ONONDAGA COUNTY ORPHAN ASYLUM.

The sad intelligence of the death of your husband was received by the managers of the Onondaga County Orphan Asylum with feelings of sorrowful regret. Mr. Leavenworth has been for nearly two decades a valued member of the Asylum's Board of Trustees, and in all deliberations of the united boards, the wisdom of his counsels was unquestioned. His life has been prolonged until he has seen nearly all the early workers with whom he was associated in this charity pass away; and now, burdened with years, and having long stood upon the border land, he, too, has joined the innumerable throng. Accept the earnest sympathy of our Board in your bereavement.

FROM W. S. LEAVENWORTH.

I was surprised and pained to learn of the death of General Leavenworth. Allow me, as one who has received many benefits at his hands, to express my sympathy for you all in this time of sorrow. He was a noble man and has set a bright example to all those who bear or may bear the name of Leavenworth. I shall always be proud that I have known him, and grateful to him for his interest in me. I shall do my best and endeavor to be a worthy representative of the name which General Leavenworth has done so much to honor.

FROM EZEKIEL W. MUNDY.

It is a pain to me to-day to learn of the death of your honored husband. He has been a most valuable man in public life and a most kind and agreeable one in private life. When I came to Syracuse twenty-five years ago, a young man and a stranger, General Leavenworth sought me out and without introduction invited me to his house, and introduced me to the people of Syracuse. And from that time onward his house was always open to me, and special invitations to meet friends there were frequent. And this kindness to me, as I know, was but a specimen of his natural courtesy. You will see, therefore, that it is but human for his friends to mourn his loss. He has, however, done much, and we should be thankful as well as sad.

www.ingramcontent.com/pod-product-compliance
Lightning Source LLC
Chambersburg PA
CBHW030026030726
47499CB00008B/3145